Spite

Anjeli Chapman Wolf

Wrong Publishing

For Zoë Matt-Williams

Table of Contents

French Turn	1
The Wizard	18
Saint Jane	26
Acknowledgments	41

Copyright © 2024 Anjeli Chapman Wolf
Cover Artwork © Zoë Matt-Williams, Mashaal Sajid

All Rights Reserved. This book, and any portion thereof, may not be reproduced, in whole or in part—except for by reviewers for the public press, and for the use of brief quotations in book reviews or educational materials—without the express permission of the publisher.

First edition, published in Canada.

French Turn

Let me tell you about your parents.

He got married at a wedding hall in the lower forties. She'd tried to snatch the bouquet and missed it. Her dress was tight and salmon-colored. He had a difficult time with the zipper.

They fucked stealthily in the coat check while the bride was busy with a flower girl who'd wrapped herself in several yards of veil and wouldn't come out.

The night that Arthur got engaged, everybody went to Bletchley's on 51st. Everyone was ruddy-faced and shouting a little when the bride-to-be got a splitting headache and hailed a cab. The party carried on. Arthur turned around to pass someone a gimlet when he found himself face-to-face with her.

Your mother's mother would have called her a jolie laide. Your father's mother would've been less charitable. She had more teeth than mouth and the aquiline nose of a Roman senator. She parted her dark hair down the middle and it clashed incongruously with the nose. Her eyes were flint-colored, but she played them up nicely with mascara and languid blinks.

"Congratulations," said Celeste. She leaned one elbow on the bar.

"Thanks."

She smiled as their friends milled around them, buffeting her back and forth. Arthur wondered idly if she was wearing a bra.

A trip beneath the kitchen stairs determined she was not. She blew him tactfully as the door above them swung open, bringing a current of angry waiters, frightened busboys and clouds of opaque steam.

He fucked her hard and quietly, her face wedged into the place where the two walls met. Afterwards, he let go of her numb arm so he could straighten his tie.

A bare bulb swayed gently in the stairwell. The light made her dark blouse lustrous, like foreign money. They smiled at each other. Then he cleared his throat and climbed the stairs.

She sauntered past him as Trip clapped him on the back and Darby spilled gin down his jacket. She collected her handbag from Betsy D. and was spirited home in the back of a taxicab. At a quarter to one, she heard the high whine of the buzzer.

She found him leaning against the doorframe, both shoes untied. One side of his collar was turned up, sticking over the lapel of his jacket like the untucked wing of a bird. A strand of sandy hair obscured his right eye.

Some shift had occurred. He shouldn't be on the fifth floor of a civilized co-op but edging furtively from the entrance of the Times Square subway to the drooping awning of the peep show. He wore the expression of urban desperation that parents describe to their children to prevent them from moving out.

He took her on the kitchen counter and elected to spend the night.

As the light crept in, she pushed the hair back fondly from Arthur's sleeping, sweaty face and traced the length of his broad nose with the tip of a finger. She'd liked him at college from a conservative distance. He'd always had a sharp jawline and his hairline hadn't jumped. Lately his stomach had acquired a layer of thin pink fat. She patted it gently.

He awoke to discover she'd gone shopping with Betsy P. but had fried him an egg and left two aspirin on the nightstand.

She slept in a wooden four-poster. Her bedroom was lined with narrow closets that were completely unused, as all her clothes were in delicate heaps on the floor.

Arthur yanked open the bedroom door and stood in the doorway with his eyes closed, scratching his stomach in a beam of light.

The living room looked like someone had left two lamps and a couch in a secondhand bookshop. Her apartment was pleasantly dirty. It was in a thin, unfashionable building. Her kitchen window had a grimy little fire escape that was freckled with gum.

He wandered around her apartment until a quarter to four. This was out of character, but it was a Saturday. He had nowhere to be. So he padded around in his socks and boxers, drinking her orange juice.

He thumbed through a paperback called *Sexual Politics*, which was dogeared and full of meaningful symbols. He was disappointed by the lack of pictures. She'd clipped a small, smudged photo of Bryan Ferry from a newspaper and taped to the bathroom mirror.

At a quarter to four, he stretched and yawned and went back home to Tilda.

Tilda had a snubbed nose and hair the color of margarine and everyone agreed she was a bit of a darling. She had no patience for absurdist comedy or surrealist art. As with all the best darlings, she was in possession of an inelastic mind.

He closed his apartment door with an elbow and threw his keys on the floor. Tilda was strewn prettily across the couch, her hair in rollers.

"Hello, you," she said, giving him an airy kiss with her eyes on the television. "Where did you end up?"

"I'm not entirely sure," he said, leaning into the fridge for the orange juice.

He'd expected a hard enquiry but apparently that was enough for Tilda.

His apartment had two bathrooms and very high ceilings but somehow Tilda made it all feel smaller. There was no conversation about Tilda moving in. It had happened by degrees when he wasn't looking. Now it seemed impolite to tell her to leave.

Since Tilda started living in his home, he'd felt that one's life amounts to little more than a list of one's routines. This thought made him feel claustrophobic, so he'd started another list. It was comprised of the little things that Tilda does not know: the additional bagel he ate when she'd left for her vague publishing job in the morning, the money he gave to the smack addict in the park. The occasional joint. Celeste.

He got ready to shower just as Tilda was taking out her curlers and wriggling into a puce suit. He watched her toss her hair in the mirror, spray it with Hold-Tite, and admire the effect from multiple angles.

In college, Tilda resembled the punks who loiter in record shops and spit on law-abiding citizens. She wore men's work boots and carried loose papers in an orange duffle bag from the Salvation Army. She attended every Vietnam protest. He had never met anyone so desperate to be pepper sprayed.

He should've been suspicious of Tilda's immaculate feathered hair, or the fact that she always ditched the frayed overalls before Christmas in Ossining. In time, the dalliance with men's footwear proved to be a diversion from her inevitable footpath. She got nervous above 96th Street. There were no more protests. Nothing made her angry anymore.

And now she turned to look at him, glancing down at his bare stomach.

"You could do with a run," she told him, smacking his stomach lightly before fastening her heavy gold earrings.

He stood with his towel around his waist as Tilda tousled his hair and departed, her heels clicking down the uncarpeted hallway. He was left gazing at his own reflection.

He took it in: the drifting cheekbones, the yellowing teeth. He was being treated like a bed object. But wasn't that wonderful, or at least enough?

He rested his elbows on the sterile marble counter and thought of his mother. She'd had wheat-colored hair and freckles which she powdered over. The morning after a party, she'd dashed the ash from her cigarette and instructed him to lie on the bathroom floor with the back of his neck rested on the cool rim of the bathtub. He'd blinked at the bright fluorescents and then closed his eyes.

Arthur had sat on the damp scraps of confetti that made their way beneath the bathroom door as she poured flat champagne over his hair.

It was called a French Turn. He remembered the stickiness, the gentle scrape of her nails against his scalp. The champagne was meant to keep him blond. It was a Parisian superstition and it hadn't worked. In a few months, his hair would darken, and she had not hidden her disappointment.

He took to his bed. By the time Tilda tripped home, he hadn't moved. She flounced into the master bathroom and then gave him a curt kiss on the head before toweling off and flicking the light off. She was not only polite but deliberately incurious.

In the morning, he rolls over to discover that she's turned like yoghurt in the night. She lies on her back, face obscured by night cream, body encased in something pink with snaps and a bodice. He edges away from her. She curls into the crook of his left armpit. The night cream drips gelatinously down his shirt.

"How'd you sleep?" she asks drowsily.

He pulls the duvet over his head and says nothing.

"Eggs?" she asks him, straightening up with a rustle of tulle and gunning for the kitchen. He burrows deeper.

He lies there, gently suffocating. Arthur can hear her banging around. If he doesn't get up, she'll call his name. He heaves himself up and shuffles in her direction.

He stands in the hallway and watches her make breakfast from a distance. She pours limp eggs on bone china painted with a mountain scene. He edges closer and stares down at the wet eggs to avoid looking at Tilda's face.

Last week, she threw out his everything scissors, which he'd used to cut the fat off bacon and trim his pubic hair.

He puts the coffee cup to his mouth. It, too, has a nasty little pattern. He feels the scrape of chipped ceramic against his front tooth as he watches Tilda spoon watery cottage cheese in a bowl. Her hair is pulled back in an earnest braid. The clink of her bangles is claxon-like. If he squints, he has only the vaguest image of her face.

His thoughts stray elsewhere.

Twenty blocks down and three to the left, the object of his thoughts has just alighted from an elevator. Celeste knocks on 301. It's eventually opened by Harrison, whose head brushes the doorframe.

Harrison is British, which allows her to overlook his more significant faults. She once drank highballs in a sling chair and watched him wrestle her brother Tandy into a headlock during a tennis match. She recalls making eye contact with Tandy, his sneakers squeaking pathetically, his lip split like a tight dress.

Harry answers the door in cigarette pants, his phone pressed between his shoulder and his ear. He gives her a kiss that lands on her jaw. A record is playing very loudly from his white sound system.

Celeste perches on the edge of his sofa and waits for him to hang up the phone. Shrill jazz ricochets around the apartment, bouncing off the corners of sharp furniture. There's no beat to dance to. She fidgets, reaching into her immaculate knot of hair and plucking out a gold pin with long fingernails. She fiddles with it, then adjusts the buckle on her shoe.

They ride to Fred and Alice's in silence, their wine bottle clinking quietly on the floor when the cab rolls to a stop at red lights.

Alice's warm breath smells like peppermint gum. Fred stinks of hamster bedding. Celeste takes care to remark on the beautifully high ceilings as they're ushered inside.

All around them are mutual friends and hangers-on, a seething mass of pink faces gesticulating and bumping into the radiator. Trip and Fern are doing the egg-beater in the living room. When the song ends, Trip pinches the front of his shirt, peeling it from his sweaty chest to fan himself.

The lights are low and cigar smoke hangs like a tropical microclimate. She glances around at the muttering fleshiness and wonders if her parents stood in this same room, furrowed the same path from the kitchen to the den like salmon, like monarch butterflies.

She turns around to find herself looking at Tilda's narrow backside. A proprietorial hand is placed on Tilda's waist.

The owner of the hand turns and catches her eye.

There is the presence then sudden absence of expression, like birds congregating and scattering from a lawn.

Celeste gives a tight smile to Tilda, whose breasts are hiked up to her chin.

Harrison leans in and kisses Tilda's cheek. Their partners say nothing. One looks at the floor, the other at the ceiling.

There's a heat in Arthur's inner ear. He meets Celeste's eyes. She smells of black pepper and cloves. Other bodies are pressing in around them, packing them into a corner with the oppressive stickiness of a Texan porch party.

He wonders if he's standing an appropriate distance from her. He considers how a man normally stands.

"Arthur," a voice intones. Chilly fingers encircle his wrist. Tilda is yanking his arm as one might yank the leash of a deaf terrier.

Harry gives his girlfriend's ankle a little kick with the heel of his shoe.

"I'm getting a drink," he says.

Celeste makes a noise in the back of her throat but doesn't look at him.

Arthur allows himself to be dragged past Darby and Trip and Carlisle, who are lolling around the mantlepiece.

Their ties are too tight, exaggerating their fat heads. Darby's moon face perches on his starched collar like an egg on a doily. The crackling fire throws Trip's syphilitic pockmarks into sharp relief. Carlisle looks passable, but when he turns into the light it's clear that his scalp is thinning.

Arthur winces at the thought that these are his people. He doesn't know anyone else.

He leans against a bust of someone's uncle and thinks of nothing. Tilda's standing resolutely with her back to him. She was ignoring him because he'd arrived at the party late and alone. Arthur could feel the pull of his fiancée somewhere in the house.

He stuffed a cigarette in his mouth and lit it on the stove. He stood in the empty kitchen, lurking in the shadow of the fridge and using a mug as an ashtray.

A war was forming in the corner of the living room. Fred and Alice's son had procured a stick from somewhere and was whacking the other children in the shins with it.

Arthur often forgot that his friends had children. The son is already walking with Fred's gait, his chest sticking out. The natural turn of his mouth is a frown.

Arthur stayed there until he was finally ousted from his post by Kathleen Whittaker, who boxed him into his position behind the fridge and started a monologue. She had bangs with the coarseness of pubic hair.

It occurred to him that he might never have a new experience.

In the middle of this revelation, he saw Celeste framed in the kitchen doorway. She was wearing a lamé jumpsuit, her dark hair piled up on her head in gleaming knots. Harrison had a hand on her bare shoulder but was addressing a meat heiress from Chicago who was draped in a dead fox and had fantastic gaps in her teeth. He was making her laugh so hard that her earrings shook. Celeste was examining a wall sconce, smoke billowing archly from the corner of her mouth.

Arthur tried to emit some soundless frequency. Her eyes didn't move from the wall sconce.

As he looked at her, he felt an atavistic instinct curling and un curling in some corner of his gut. He watched Celeste stretch, her shoulder blades rolling as she raised her arms and let out a shameless yawn.

He felt that he was on the verge of discovering something, that there was some secret of the universe beckoning at him with its hand extended. But that had been twenty minutes ago, and now he's sequestered in the drawing room, looking at the back of Tilda's head.

He notices that every woman wears her hair clipped back in the same way. He wants to remark on this to Tilda but when he pokes her shoulder, he discovers the woman beside him is actually Tiffy. He should've known: her shoes are a lighter shade of orange.

Arthur begins edging along the hallway. His hair slickens with sweat. He needs to eat something that isn't a cocktail onion. He looks for his fiancée.

But in a moment of beautiful convenience, he cannot find her. Every woman is an almost-Tilda.

His mouth fills with saliva. His legs walk away with him.

Outside, he turns his collar up. Snow drifts into the crosswalk and sits there sourly.

Arthur squints across the street at a man in a denim jacket who's rocking peacefully on the opposite curb. The man's collar is turned down. He has high cheekbones and hair to his shoulders. He lifts his chin, blinking purely up at heaven.

Arthur stares. The man is barefoot, his toes curling around the curb like the lip of a diving board. Arthur, his hair plastered wetly against his forehead, considers the interior life of a man like that.

Arthur doesn't move. The light turns.

The man walks towards him, the hem of his jeans scraping wet ground. As he reaches Arthur, the corners of his mouth turn up in a very gentle smile.

Arthur reaches out with a dime.

As Arthur stretches out his hand, the dime falls from his palm. It lands on a patch of bare pavement sheltered beneath a dented street sign.

The dime lands on its edge. It balances there. Arthur stares down at it.

"That's how you know it's a simulation," says the man. He smiles wider and doesn't pick up the dime.

Arthur opens his mouth, but the man has walked past him, stepping through snow. Perhaps for the first time, Arthur realizes there are other ways to be.

He turns to see the man's back, hoping for another revelation. Red felt letters have been clumsily sewn to his denim jacket. But the letters are illegible, or in Arabic.

Arthur remains turned, his head twisted on his neck, waiting at the light as it changes and changes again.

Celeste had let her eyes follow Arthur as he wandered out of the foyer and shut the door. Then she catches herself and crosses her eyes instead, focusing on the cherry of her cigarette.

"When are you getting married, Harry?" says someone in the next room.

Harrison laughs. "To who?"

"Well, Celeste."

Harrison's voice drops to a stage whisper. She edges closer to the door but hears nothing but laughter. Celeste stands in the middle of the hallway, impeding traffic like a blocked, conspicuous pore.

She peeks around the lip of the doorframe and watches Harrison. He grips the stem of his glass in a fist and gulps wine with his mouth open. She imagines the genital pink interior of his throat opening and closing as he swallows.

Harrison didn't want to marry her. She did not particularly want to marry him but would've relished the opportunity to say so. She'd rather atrophy alone under stacks of periodicals and taxidermy.

But Harry had met her mother. She'd been wrapped in a blue silk robe and matching turban, sitting up in bed for once and gripping his arm with one suddenly bony hand.

That robe is now crumpled in the corner of Celeste's room. She can feel it eyeing her as she undresses for bed.

Celeste's mother hadn't wanted her married as much as she'd wanted her future to be visible, known: toast on a plate. The ease with which Harry patted her mother's thigh made it clear he was a known quantity.

Celeste considers how many unknown quantities she's ignored.

A beautifully tall man once cornered her at a party and asked her if she'd like to take ecstasy and go through a car wash. She'd coughed loudly and then, uncertain of what to do next, pretended to be foreign and excused herself.

For seven years, Harry has been over her shoulder, eating her youth with a spoon. But now she gives a little shiver and approaches.

She comes close to him, her earrings swaying, a little sweat on her upper lip.

He can see something missing behind her eyes, some absent piece. He's still clutching the stem of his glass in his left fist.

He stares into her face at that emptiness, that lack.

What had she ever been hoping for? That he would change? That she'd beat the roving eye out of him as if he were a crêpe paper piñata?

How would she have done that? With what tools? With her wit and charm?

She hadn't fooled herself into thinking that he'd stop flirting with cigarette girls, with her younger sister. But she had decided, somehow, that this was fine. This was as well as she'd ever do.

She's not sure what they were laughing about. It doesn't matter.

Shame creeps like a sunburn across her nose. She says nothing, only holding his gaze and swallowing and then, finally, walking sedately out.

After six blocks, she deduces that someone is following her. She musters a glare and turns around, but it's only Harrison, moping openly under an awning, too tall to hide.

"Peanut!" Harry shouts.

The peanut in question is already flouncing off.

Harry trails her lamely, drizzle sliding off the grease in his hair. She's looking fixedly at a neon advertisement for nylon stockings. A blinking orange woman, thirty feet in the air, rolls her stockings steadily up her thigh, then down, then up.

"It was a joke and a poor one. I'm a fool of the lowest order. Am I forgiven? Am I?"

He almost means this. He did feel quite badly when he saw her march out. She's also got his house keys in her purse.

There is more to life than mothering someone else's pale son. She does not turn around but saunters away, dodging puddles.

Across town, Arthur is lying face down on his bed as the sun begins to creep through the window. His left eye is pressing painfully against the braided edge of a pillow. When he's married, he'll spend all his evenings being dragged around like a funfair goldfish.

He's never wanted children. A baby is just another bald-headed accolade, too large for the mantlepiece. Tilda is obsessed with children. She will grab his arm hard at lunch to point out the rolls of fat on a passing toddler.

The thought of engaging in a binding contract with this harridan gives him spots on the edge of his vision. He'd go to work and she would live in his house, spending his money on frilly household peripherals.

Whatever complex mechanism kept his ancestors alive and breeding is starting to falter within him.

He will not, he decides, become his father.

His thoughts stray again to Celeste, who seems far too wry and angular to want kids. He wonders if she's on birth control.

Celeste would've let him keep his everything scissors.

The next morning will find him in Celeste's apartment, having charmed her doorman and unearthed the key beneath her mat. She's out, but not for long. The front door will soon swing open.

She stands in the doorway in a lavender skirt and matching loafers. They gaze at each other, his face unwashed and unshaven. He's already taken off his shirt and doesn't shield his softened stomach.

Her face cracks into a grin and she tosses her bag on the rug.

Later, after she's pushed her skirt back down, she rolls sideways on the couch until her head is resting lightly in his lap. She gives a little chirp, like a radio turning on. She moves the pad of her index finger across his eyebrow. The gesture gives him a pleasurable shiver until he shrugs her off. When they exit her apartment in separate directions, he'll realize it threw him because it was entirely unstudied.

He thinks of the future. They might have nothing in common but a shared malady. But when he kisses her, he feels the sensation of going north.

It occurs to him that she is his doom. She wasn't always his, but he's always had one. Today it wears her face.

He decides that they're blameless.

And so he allows it. They spend late April and all of May eating grease in distasteful parts of the Village, feeding on each other's mouths in alleyways. They visit galleries in oversized sunglasses. They are never recognized.

They spend one Saturday night in a damp basement, watching a drag show in which every act wears the same pink wig, tossing it back and forth to scattered applause.

The wedding is set for the ninth of June. Time continues to shuffle its feet down the hallway.

The church smells of rotting wood. Vases vomit white gardenias. He raises his eyeline so that he can't see Tilda proceeding slowly towards him from the other end of the room.

The Wizard

A woman is tramping through the graying snow in the wizard's driveway. He watches her through his blinds.

Gillian came to find the wizard because she's heard tales of his wit and valor. The tales are old. When she arrives at his door, there's a note written on the back of a receipt. *No Longer Performing or Removing Spells, Enchantments.*

Wizards are immortal. They are immune to death. But they are not immune to everything.

The wizard has spent most of the last quarter century in bed. He lies in a nest of blankets. There is something rotting. He can smell it but is ignorant to its origins.

He finally hears the insistent hiss of the doorbell.

The wizard opens the door calmly, his blanket draped around his shoulders like a robe. He's not sure if his crying was audible. There's a chance he won't have to explain himself.

The wizard has stringy black hair that reaches his collar. His glasses are greasy and perfectly round, balancing precipitously on the edge of his nose. He looks up at Gillian, feeling for the pale Band-Aid that's losing its hold on the back of his neck.

To enter his apartment, Gillian must step over a towering pile of unread mail that's collected on the plastic mat. Some of it's decades old, magazines that have already flourished and folded.

The wizard grew up in Akron. If pressed, he says he stayed because he likes it.

This was never true. He has a physical aversion to the squat apartment block where his mother raised him, the freeway, the high school with its concrete steps and frigid sophomores.

His father had been a low-budget magician. He'd wear a dinner jacket and catch fake bullets in his teeth. He did card tricks, but not good ones. He billed himself as The Great Zambini, although he wasn't billed often. He was not a wizard. His parlor tricks fooled only the nearsighted.

His most successful trick was a vanishing act.

People think that wizards create magic. But magic is already out there, fording rivers, galloping across fens. It is looking for a conduit.

The wizard was endowed with the power of prophecy. His gifts become apparent at the age of five. He is sitting on the floor of the living room, building a trembling tower of blocks. At any moment, it could fall into the merciless sea of the carpet. The blinds are raised and sunlight is dribbling in.

In his father's absence, his mother has started going to hairdressing school. She's already given herself a hideous amateur perm. She straightens the collar of her jean jacket and reaches down to rest a hand on her son's shoulder. But as his mother bends near him, the little wizard grips her arm.

"You snip away dead cells on the heads of happier people."

"What?" she says, one eye on the clock on the kitchen wall.

"When you leave this house and walk to your car, you are going to be hit by a long-haul truck delivering frozen meat to Cincinnati."

He turns back to his blocks. He'd grabbed her so tightly that when he releases her, one of her bangles leaves a pink imprint on her wrist.

She steps backwards, her breathing shallow. She studies her son, who's gone back to building his little block tower. He's wearing his navy corduroy overalls, his legs splayed into a tiny V. As she watches him, he rests both hands on his knees and frowns at the tower.

Keys, purse, gum. She shifts her weight from foot to foot. *Fish fingers in freezer.*

She would have blamed his outburst on too much late-night television, but they've pawned it. She brushes the gentle suede of her skirt with a thumb. There is a throbbing sore inside her cheek.

The whole room is now bathed in light. It makes his hair even blonder. She looks at the back of his sunny head as he sits there, absorbed by his blocks. He wiggles his feet, curling his bare toes into the white shag of the carpet.

She adjusts the strap of her purse, laughs, and collects her keys from the decorative seashell on her way out the door.

Prophetic abilities need tuning, like new antenna. She is only run over by a bike and her injuries are minor.

After the prophecy came flight, then extrasensory perception. At 15, the wizard experienced a horrible growth spurt and with it a variety of strange abilities. He suddenly found himself levitating his toast at breakfast. He coughed and set his sister on fire.

He always knew when he was about to time travel because his gums would bleed. For many years, this was his favorite gift. What bliss to be elsewhere. But the wizard has crippling social anxiety, no matter the century.

There's a grainy photograph of him standing between George and Patti Harrison. He leans awkwardly on the mantlepiece, wearing clothes that haven't been invented yet.

For a while, the wizard was happy, or at least occupied.

But as he grew older, his abilities became natural extensions of himself, like a cigarette holder or stilts. He became used to predicting death or economic collapse and keeping it to himself.

He could predict the outcome of a relationship before it started. He might see a woman perched on a bar stool. She'll bend over to adjust her shoelace and a pack of Virginia Slims will fall out of her shirt pocket.

He will know that her mother smoked Virginia Slims. He'll concentrate harder and see that she was raised Irish Catholic, lost her sister, waxes her legs. She has always dreamed of settling down in a cottage by a body of salt water. He knows what she likes.

And so, with his own little stutters and flourishes, he regurgitates it back to her. But there is no pulse to this. He's following a script.

This is not to suggest that he has never been in love. He has, desperately. But when the wizard receives the love of other people, he's never sure where to put it. Better to stay at home and watch redheads do handstands, or whatever he does on the internet.

Magic arrived before good and evil, before being and nonbeing. God gave us grain. Bread is inevitable. But there's a right way to wield magic, by curing headaches and engaging in neighborly acts.

Lately the wizard wonders if this is just something that wizards tell themselves. Summoning cats from trees raises no philosophical quandaries. If wizards never do anything, then they never do anything wrong.

His goodly deeds have been wholly accidental, like the day he sneezed with his wand in his pocket and cast a beam of righteous light that blinded a gunman who'd infiltrated the House of Parliament. This resulted in some very nice press for the wizard. But it was unearned and quickly dissipated. The wizard didn't photograph well.

Gillian had seen the old photos, had read about the wizard's OBE. He'd been hard to find, but she found him. Gillian adjusts her scrunchie and sits. Her dark hair curls into her eyes. Her pink sweater is sticking to her.

She is here on a critical errand. Her husband, Dan, is dying. He was a lifelong smoker and now breathes through a hole in his neck. But she was a smoker, too, and will live a long and unencumbered life, neck intact.

Gillian is not aware that her mother made this same journey in 1987.

Gillian's mother was named Ethel. Ethel had stood on the doormat in tight shoes and, when he finally answered the door, wafted a cloud of hairspray into the wizard's apartment. In 1987, the wizard had been more relaxed about cigarette burns in the rug. The coffee table scooched over and offered her an ashtray.

She'd sat on the edge of his couch, exhaled a rotten cloud and cracked her knuckles.

"I'm here about—" Ethel began.

But the wizard had looked up at her balefully from the rim of a mug of Tang and she'd faltered. He'd met her gaze and held it.

He'd known what she was here about. It was the same reason that Ethel's mother had come to him in 1964.

Ethel's mother Claire wore a soft pink skirt that matched her pocketbook. When she rang the doorbell, he'd been in the middle of making himself a gimlet. She'd leaned against the kitchen doorway and watched him cut a lime with a breadknife, saying nothing, raising one heavily penciled eyebrow.

Gillian was the third generation to come to the wizard. Like her mother, and her mother before, each married to men with fatal smoking habits.

He'd tacked a few years onto the lives of various husbands by advising menthols or hypnosis. The husbands would wheeze around the house for a few more years, spawning children. The children would creep out of the house at night to fall in love with other smokers.

Gillian knows how she would like to die: in an opera dress, slumped down in a comfortable armchair beside the man she loves. Perhaps there's the distant ring of the nicest of her nieces on the phone.

She'd like to have just arrived from somewhere, her shoes only just removed. She would not like to wake up alive and find her husband expired in the opposite chair, shuffling off his mortal coil while she slept.

She doesn't want to be left behind.

They have no children, although she'd like some. At thirty-eight, she'd expected more than a toy poodle with cataracts. And Dan deserves to live a little more. He's always patient, always apologetic. Even with the neck hole, he still does the dishes.

The wizard regards her through puffy lids. He looks at her as he reaches into the waistband of his stained pajamas to scratch his lower back.

He can tell, with this cursory glance, that she could live to 105. He knows that Dan could die next weekend. In August, Chariot the poodle will take advantage of an open door, run into the street, and get squashed beneath the wheel of a laundry van. If he tells Gillian to keep her doors locked, the dog will be a fixture on her couch until March of 2026.

Prophets have the power to change the very future they predict. The wizard, for instance, knows that Dan is doing the dishes because he thinks his death is imminent. But the wizard is aware of a new treatment that could extend Dan's life by twenty years.

Something happens to people who are sudden recipients of stolen decades. Sometimes they decide to mountain bike.

In Dan's case, the result is more predictable. He'll file for divorce six weeks after leaving the hospital. He'll die in the arms of a frizzy-haired steakhouse waitress.

Gillian scratches her knee and settles back into the stiff couch.

The wizard visualizes all the possible pathways of her life. He can see them in his mind, spread out in intricate patterns with multi-colored paths of intersecting light, like a glorious subway map. He sees the forks in each path, marking his own interventions.

Of all possible worlds, there is only one that does not end in alcoholism or violent suicide.

The wizard performs his greatest feat of magic and turns her into a Catholic church.

Initially, the church is very upset, because it still has the memories of being a woman with ambitions and legs. But gradually those memories fade, replaced by recollections of bright flashes of color and curtains of sounds and smells, like the remembrance of one's infancy.

It is a 17th century Italian church, nestled in the outskirts of Florence, with tall spires and an intact pipe organ.

And the church has fêtes and mass and baptisms. In the summer months, there are weddings. There is music and beautiful lights strung up from the balustrades and a fund to fix a hole in the church's roof.

This is where her lineage ends.

Dan worries about his missing wife, but not too much. After an appropriate period, he meets and marries the waitress.

The church is never lonely and gradually begins to forget the meaning of the word.

Saint Jane

To her left is an asthmatic second cousin. To her right is a balding uncle who keeps shifting in his chair, sweat collecting in the band of his tight watch.

It's a bad table.

The cake has already been cut. The stem of the wine glass is feeling a little thin in her fist. It must be time to leave.

Jane walks down a path of crumbling red brick, dodging Evelyn's friends. At the end of the path, she glances back.

Intricate lace crawls up Evelyn's neck. Jane stands very still and watches Evelyn swallow a mouthful of water. Then Jane turns, pushes hard on the wrought iron gate with her shoulder, and walks out.

Jane stands for hours at the station in the warm gut of the sunset. Finally, the sun dips and her bare knees start to freeze. The train inches in, late. She boards, sits, and lurches delicately as it pulls away. As she untangles her wool scarf from her mouth, she shifts forward sharply.

There is a blurry figure running through the dry field to her left. It's the size of a man, hunched over and hurtling through the dusk, matching pace with the train.

Her breath quickens and she draws closer before realizing it's a smudge on the window.

Jane peels off her gel nails one by one in perfect, intact pieces and puts them in the pocket of her cardigan.

She isn't living with her parents. She was, but she isn't anymore.

Several people at the wedding want to know how her parents are doing. The answer is *too well*. They're seeing films on weeknights. They are inexplicably vegan.

They installed a grab bar in the shower. It's not the ugly plastic kind but a sleek, Scandinavian one. For some reason, she found its presence offensive and told them so. Her parents blinked and asked if she wanted them to slip in the shower and die.

Of course not.

But now she is living in North Carolina with her maiden aunt. Gertie's seventy-eight and so pale that she's nearly invisible. Her house is cream-colored, with turrets and splintering floors. Jane lives in the room above the garage, surrounded by boxes of memorabilia. She sleeps on a narrow brass bed and bathes irregularly in a clawfoot tub coated in white plaque.

Gertie's wedding dress was made entirely of gossamer and could be folded up to fit in a standard envelope. This was how the dress was delivered in 1976. The sealed envelope is perched on a towering pile of detritus in Jane's room. There's a story there, but Jane lacks the energy to ask.

Gertie grows roses in the cupboard beneath the sink. They flourish beneath a dim bulb. She clips the rosehips and brew them into the gray distillate that she drinks every night by the glow of the television.

The cabinet over Gertie's sink is full of expired medication. There are rows of capped prescriptions for glaucoma and gout. Most are unopened. This is apparently what the distillate is for.

Jane had shown up early on a Wednesday, shifting from foot to foot with her belongings stuffed in a plastic bag. She hadn't called.

The bus ride had been sticky. She'd rung the doorbell, which made a distant fizzing whine. She could hear shuffling in some far corner of the house and waited, the bag swinging loosely in one hand.

The door had swung open to reveal Gertie, her eyes like pool water, a small frame with a sharply upright spine. The joints of her elbows and knees bulged beneath taught skin. Between the hem of her dress and the floor, her large bare feet protruded like skis.

Gertie had opened the door wide and then stepped back, as if Jane were not only expected but late.

They rarely speak. The only person Jane talks to at length is her therapist, a sympathetic woman with hairy knuckles.

"So," the therapist will begin, picking lint off a beige sweater that clings to her middle. Jane finds herself exhaling slowly and gazing at the childish sketch of a sailboat on the opposite wall.

The therapist's waiting room has one armchair in a stain-free color and a dusty plastic fern. There is one door for patients to enter the office and another door for them to exit to the warm parking lot, with its fungal smell of trash.

It is one of two rooms in which Jane encounters a mirror. It's rimmed with white plastic and too big to avoid, so Jane confronts it immediately. The door shuts behind her with the sound of a cracked knuckle.

She's wearing a yellow shirt that says *Oklahoma!* and basketball shorts that meet her knees. Her dark hair now reaches all the way down her back. It's still parted down the middle.

But the face in the mirror is pallid. The eyebrows seem sparser. There are soft pink scabs around the mouth. She sticks out her tongue and is surprised to find it white and clouded.

Her therapist asks if she's considered dating. This is a constant refrain. Some friends will even brave the trip south, sitting on stiff chairs in Gertie's kitchen and squinting compassionately across the table. She can see them pretending they cannot smell the curtains or see the oil leaking from a lower cabinet. It drips steadily onto the floor as they offer her the sons of their chiropractors.

She balks at the suggestion. Depending on her mood, it's either been too long or not long enough.

After therapy, she bikes to the grocery store. She and Gertie split the social security check that comes on the third of the month. This means they buy store-brand cereal and their meat must be purchased in bulk. The austerity feels pleasantly monastic.

She needs glasses that she doesn't wear. Everything more than twenty feet away becomes a warm blur. The grocery store is a fuzzy mash of color and shape. She squints before gathering armfuls of wet chicken breasts and generic toilet paper. She shuffles down the aisle quickly, her slippers flapping at her heels. She wipes her nose and blinks and only later, when she's emptied her arms onto the conveyer belt, she registers what she's seen.

There was a face peering out between the tins of tomato paste.

She bikes slowly. This isn't just because of her vision. If she rushed, she'd find herself home too soon, lying on her brass bed for an extra hour. The cracked paint on her ceiling is looking more and more like a rabbit.

To her right is a field of decaying corn. On her left is a vast expanse of soy. The cardboard pint of milk in her bicycle basket thunks softly as she rides over uneven patches of asphalt.

At home, she gazes at her reflection in the mirror of the medicine cabinet for a quarter of an hour before popping her zits without satisfaction.

Jane has started to remember her dreams. Two weeks after her arrival, she awoke in the middle of the night to find the walls had been replaced with dark green tarp. The tarp walls were identical to the real ones except the tarp would waver at the corners, almost imperceptibly.

But in the morning the walls were walls.

Eight nights after that, she'd rolled over to find herself face to face with two waxy yellow goblins in smocks. They were as tall as her nightstand and they were pushing a metal gurney across her room, grunting quietly with the effort. Their smocks were grubby. They paused before her bedroom door, as if determining the logistics of getting the gurney into the hallway.

She shifted and her sheets made an audible rustling. One of the goblins turned to look at her, his face suddenly illuminated as if a candle was beneath his chin. He had the tight, weathered skin of an aging rockstar.

In the morning, her door was ajar.

Tonight, she falls asleep in the usual way. She dreams of childhood friends, their faces blurry and misremembered except for Sybil. Sybil had thin brown hair and furrowed eyebrows.

She and Sybil liked to talk about God. Jane didn't know much about God, so this meant that Sybil would tell her about the Flood and Lot's wife while they stood at the bus stop, tugging up their socks. To love God, said Sybil, is to fear Him.

Jane rolls over, her head still busy with dream, and finds something crouching on her desk. Jane recoils and draws her covers closer, staring at this apparition that hunches on all fours like a pale gargoyle, its shoes leaving marks on her unread magazines. It's wearing Sybil's Catholic school uniform, a long gray skirt and a jam-colored blazer.

But the skirt is suddenly too small. White thighs jut out, connecting to spindly shins encased in socks that were once knee-high. They now strain to swallow the ankles of whatever's perched on the desk. The blazer arrives only at the crooks of the arms, shoulder blades straining at the back of it.

The thing that wears Sybil's uniform drums its fingers against the desk. Its hair swings in front of its face, obscuring its features.

And even though it's been nearly two years, Jane reaches unconsciously for the other side of the bed, clutching for a non-existent hand.

The thing notices this gesture. From behind the curtain of hair, Jane can see a thin smile.

That's cute.

"He would've done that, too," she tells it quietly.

Actually, it tells her, *David didn't need you.*

She stares as the thing gives its head a shake and flexes its wrists.

He didn't, it repeats, allowing itself a little stretch.

Jane swallows, then opens her mouth. But it anticipates her question.

He was still in love with Margaret. They were going to elope in a national park and have the ceremony on the lip of a canyon.

Margaret was David's college girlfriend. Her hair fell in perfect, natural ringlets.

"Why are you saying this?"

I'm not telling you anything, it says, enunciating every syllable, *That you don't already know.*

She can't ask him. These are the fights they cannot have.

She had gone through his internet history afterwards. "Vacation spots in Pacific Northwest" and "backpacking Washington." He'd never mentioned wanting to camp in Washington before. She thought this might be a telling clue. Possibly he'd had a mistress in Seattle who hiked and wore scrunchies.

But he'd probably mentioned Washington when she hadn't been listening.

Before they'd moved in together, David used to stay over in her hideous pre-war with bars on the windows. He'd make her toast, unbidden, and do a little dance when he brought it to her room.

By their third year together, he was developing a gentle roundness in his lower stomach that peaked shyly over the edge of his boxers. He had a smattering of freckles on his nose and the hair on his arms was gold.

They'd gone camping only once, for two nights in Big Sur. She'd bought a soft white fleece that was almost too warm to be usable. On the first night, they couldn't start a fire. On the second, David sat in the ash of the fire pit for twenty minutes.

She'd been on the verge of bundling herself into their tent when he suddenly leapt backwards. A fire was dancing incongruously among the ashes.

He sat down heavily on a log with the expression of someone who's performed a minor miracle. In the firelight, David's hair was blonder, the hair of a child. She wriggled next to him and put her head on his shoulder. He rested a large hand on her thigh. The redwoods produced impossible shadows.

She thought, from his slow breathing, that he'd fallen asleep. The only noise was the crack of distant twigs and the soft exhale from his nose.

She'd met the people who were moving into their apartment. The realtor had tactfully scheduled the walkthrough for a time when Jane was meant to be at work. But she'd woken up late, looked out the foggy window and decided to call in sick.

She'd bumped into the new couple on the stairs as she was dragging herself to the bagel shop in odd socks. The woman had shiny chestnut hair and heeled loafers. The man smiled and small crinkles formed around his eyes. Their energy suggested that they wanted to impress the realtor and not the other way around. Maybe their credit scores were low.

But the apartment wasn't in great condition, either. The radiator didn't turn down.

When she comes back from the bathroom, the thing wearing Sybil's uniform is still on the desk, scratching the flaking skin on its left knee.

For three days, she wakes up to this pale arachnoid squatting on the arm of her chair or perched on the mantelpiece, idly kicking its legs, fiddling with the buckle on its mary janes. It scrounges around in the drawers, subsisting on a diet of old batteries and foreign currency. Its belches smell like incense.

After a few months without David, she'd found a dusty magazine in a used bookstore. She'd shuffled out of her apartment in only her winter coat and sweatpants, her face and hair unwashed. The magazine was entitled *Rites and Rituals*. On its cover was a disembodied hand clutching a perfect apple.

She'd thumbed through it in the aisle, questing. She'd flicked past rituals for attracting lovers, past spells to grow your hair. And then Jane found the page she'd been looking for. She'd repeated the incantation to herself and shut the book.

And that night, sitting on her bed in the glow of a stubby candle, she had prayed to the god of lost things. But all she'd found were single earrings. She'd misplaced them on buses and she'd thrown out their partners. But here they were, showing up mutinously in old coats and the bottoms of purses.

She leaves Gertie's to get away from the slender ghoul that's balanced on the edge of her desk. It has found the plastic container of her single earrings. It's plucking them up with two fingers and placing them on its tongue like sardines.

She bikes around in a clumsy loop from Gertie's house to the hardware store. The sky is overcast. If it rains, the droplets will be warm.

She bikes past wheat fields, which tower over her and move in tandem with every shifting breeze. The wheat stretches as far as she can see without her glasses, blurring into a yellow mist at the edges of her vision.

Jane stays inside that night and watches black-and-white movies about hard-boiled detectives. Everyone is cheating on everyone. Gertie sidles up behind her in the dark. She's chewing on something that smells like a peppermint.

During an ad break, Jane opens the bathroom door to discover the almost-Sybil sitting on the rim of the sink. It has grown, its head now pressing against the ceiling, forcing its neck to bend. Jane stares. It's playing a dulcimer but stops abruptly when she opens the door.

You ever think about getting married? it asks her, tossing the dulcimer in the sink with a clang. Hair obscures its eyes but Jane can see its mouth stretching unnaturally far across its cheeks.

She edges away, but it continues. It's obviously been waiting for her. *You do*, it says, almost flirtatiously. *You want a little saviour with a good chin.*

It cracks its pale neck in one direction, then the other.

You could get married. You could, it says, pretending to size her up.

What are you, twenty-nine? Go back to the city. Get married. It narrows its eyes. *Love will bleed you white. It will drag you backwards screaming. There are untold universes. In every one, you return to a sweet and fetal state. Alone.*

It lets out an unsuitably deep chuckle.

But me? I'm not going anywhere. Write my name in your will. Leave all your money under the counter at the third Arby's you encounter travelling south. When you die, I'll be there.

It nods again.

Count on it.

She shuts the door carefully and elects to pee in the garden. There is something lurking in the weeds.

Jane takes the stairs two at a time to avoid encountering anything else on the way to her room. She lies on her bed and looks up at the ceiling rabbit, which is holding a carrot in two fingers like a cigar.

She clicks off the light and her mind wanders out of her head and above her, like a balloon.

David fell in a spruce trap. She didn't ski and he'd kissed her with a cold, pink nose before snapping on his helmet and clomping away, poles over one shoulder. She'd been sitting in the lodge with a Styrofoam cup of hot chocolate when the lift operator had made a beeline for her, pushing up his goggles and kneeling down. The strap of his goggles had made his hair stand straight up. It was white-blond from peroxide and she found herself looking at it instead of listening to him.

A spruce trap is the space beneath a tree that is protected from snow. The branches stop powder from falling in the hollow around the base. The rest of the snow falls above that empty scoop, concealing it.

If the snow is deep enough, it creates a well. A skier can slide gamely down the mountain, unaware, and the pressure of his body can awaken the spruce trap. He will suddenly find himself eaten by a little pocket in the snow. He'll usually fall headfirst and be found in the same position, his body surrounded by tightly packed powder. His feet might alert Search and Rescue to his position because they will still be in their skis, poking out of the snowbank.

She found this out later on the internet. She'd been too busy looking at the lift operator's hair and the pink sunburn around his goggle line.

But back in their apartment, she'd used their desktop to learn what a spruce trap was, to imagine how his last moments must have felt. Maybe his skis thrashed around while he suffocated. Rapid movement packs the snow in tighter.

Possibly he screamed.

She could taste the snow in her mouth. She'd powered down their desktop and curled up over the covers, because he had made the bed and she didn't want to ruin it.

She isn't aware of falling asleep. She crawls out of bed at noon, the sun too high, her head already aching. She's started to sleep too much and urinate infrequently.

Her room is empty. It still reeks strongly of incense.

There is ash in her brain, inhibiting her from rational thought.

She opens the medicine cabinet and decides to take something purple that treats optical confusion and a red, square pill for bone disease.

Jane takes her toast outside. She sits up stiffly in the plastic chair. The pills are in Jane's palm when she feels breath on the back of her neck. She turns. Gertie, barefoot in a fluttering nightgown, is looking down at her.

Jane says nothing. She has hurriedly stuffed the pills beneath her tongue. She gazes up at Gertie. Gertie offers no expression. They stare at each other until a street lamp across the road turns on. As if this is some signal to Gertie, she reaches for the screen door to the kitchen, her nightdress whipping around the corner, leaving Jane alone.

She crosses her legs, with some effort, and gazes ruminatively over the hedgerows that separate Gertie's yard from the neighbors'. They have two little girls with long brown hair and matching corduroy jackets. They always stand their bikes up carefully against the garden shed before they go inside.

It occurs to her that she would've liked children.

She decides, sitting in her plastic chair, that she will die. Not in some distant future, but soon. She has lost her will. Her muscles will atrophy. Buzzards will peel off her flesh.

But this is wishful thinking. There's nothing wrong with her.

She sweats. The sweat dries.

She's thinking now with a clean brain, a chalkboard that has been sponged clean. She lolls backward a little in her chair.

And then she lolls forward into somewhere else.

She is on her knees in the middle of a lightless forest. The canopy above her interlocks like the roof of a cathedral. The dark trees beside her are impossibly wide and swollen with water, their branches seeking upwards to a light she cannot see.

This is nothing. This is just a larger, more elaborate apparition. She shifts her weight and the sticks on the forest floor press painfully into her knees. She hears a snuffling noise and turns, expecting an animal.

But there is a man crouched among the roots of the tree beside hers.

He's naked. His skin is the color of turned milk and every vein on his neck is visible. His blond head is drooping to his chest.

But of course, she would know him anywhere.

The gentle rounding of his stomach is still there, the same light chest hair, the firm thighs from years on a bicycle. But he suddenly looks devoid of blood. If she touched his arm, it would feel wet, amphibian.

She calls but is aware that no sound leaves her mouth. She looks down at her hands. There's only a slight shimmering, a displacement of air.

All the same, he raises his head.

There are deep gouges where his eyes should be. They've been scooped neatly from his head, as if by the talons of an enormous bird.

She calls to him again and he folds like a deck chair.

He stays there, fetal, as she crawls to him on hands and knees.

She presses her back against their tree, silent, breathing. She watches the leaves on the lower branches of the opposite pine.

After a few minutes, he raises himself. He places his palms upwards on his lap, his head loose on his neck.

They sit side by side. His head is nearly resting on her shoulder. She thinks she can hear a telephone. Maybe it's a ringing in her ears.

"Did you want me here?" she asks, shifting onto one shoulder so that she can see him properly. After a moment, he relaxes, lifting his chin to the canopy above them.

He says nothing.

Far in the distance, a bird trills and another bird responds.

Acknowledgments

An immense thank you to my family: my parents Wid and Rita, my brothers Kiran and Skyler. Thank you to the brilliant friends who have read my work: Vidya Divakaran, Miranda Fayne, Nick Bartlett, and Zoë Matt-Williams. Without Saul Barrett, this anthology would be festering in a bin. Thank you for everything. You are heaven in shoes.

About the Author

Anjeli Chapman is a writer from New York City. She lives in London. SPITE is her first anthology.

Support indie authors!

Rate it on Goodreads and get **20% off**
your next *Wrong Publishing* title

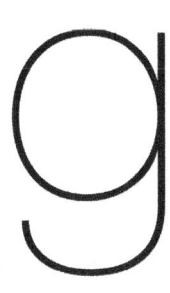

Printed in Great Britain
by Amazon